EMOTES!™

A-NET
(THE MENTOR)

THE CREATION

When the emotion of all Internet users came together, a new super-energy was created. This energy split into unique beings, each of which represents a different emotion. They are the Emotes!

SUPER
(THE CONFIDENT)

JOI
(THE EXCITED)

ABASH
(THE EMBARRASSED)

YAWNI
(THE BORED)

ICK
(THE DISGUSTED)

MIXY
(THE CONFUSED)

BUBBA
(THE HAPPY)

CANT
(THE FRUSTRATED)

BOOM
(THE ANGRY)

JUMPI
(THE SHOCKED)

IM
(THE MISCHIEVOUS)

DRAIN
(THE EXHAUSTED)

Abash and the Cyber-Bully

By Matt Casper and Ted Dorsey

Evergrow Ltd.

Hong Kong — Los Angeles

www.Emotes.com

ISBN 13:   978-988-17-3421-1

Printed in China

Abash jumped out of bed and dressed for school. "I hope today is going to be a nice, ordinary day," he said to himself.

Abash brushed his teeth, ate a bowl of Cyber-Flakes, and gulped down a glass of juice. Then he grabbed his backpack and headed out the door.

Abash jumped on his hover board and took off
toward school. But the hover board kept turning
left. "I can't turn right!" Abash shouted.
Then he crashed into a cyber-tree.

Luckily, the only one who had seen him fall was a cyber-gopher.

Abash looked at his feet and realized something strange. He was wearing two left shoes!

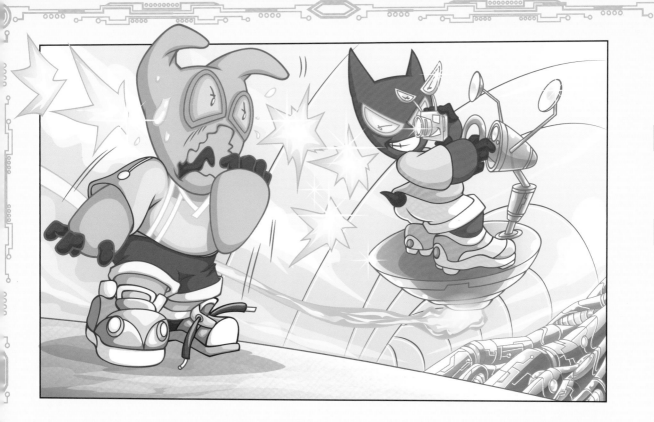

"Hey, Lefty! Smile for the camera!" It was Imp!

"Please don't show anyone, Imp!" Abash begged him. "Will you erase that picture?"

"Sure thing, whatever," Imp shouted, taking off on his rocket bike.

Watch out for me and my camera.

I'll capture you when you least expect it!

Abash picked up his hover board and began walking to school. He was very late, and the fact that his two left shoes made him go in circles wasn't helping.

Meanwhile, in the school library, Imp was busy uploading the picture of Abash. He wanted to have one last laugh at his friend's two left shoes. Suddenly, the buzzer sounded. Imp rushed off. He was late!

When Abash finally made it to school, class had already begun. Luckily, no one noticed his shoes.

By lunchtime, Abash had completely forgotten about the picture Imp had taken of him. He sat down to eat with some of his Emote friends.

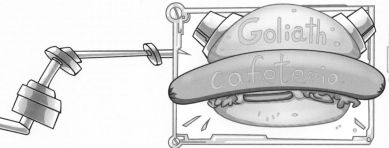

"Hey, Abash, can you dance?" asked Joi.

"I guess so. Why?" replied Abash.

"I was wondering if it's hard to dance with two left feet!" Joi exclaimed, showing everyone the picture. All the Emotes had a big laugh.

"I've heard that two *wrongs* don't make a right, but what about two *lefts*?" joked Ick. Everyone laughed again.

Abash was so embarrassed that he ran out of the cafeteria.

As he raced toward the playground, Abash glanced at the plasma screens in the hallway. There was a picture of his two left feet on every screen!

"I don't get it. Why are you wearing two left shoes?" asked Mixy, shoving the photo into Abash's hands. In the bottom corner was the word "**eXPLosion221**."

eXPLosion221

"That must be an email address. I am gonna get to the bottom of this right now," Abash muttered. He dashed toward the library.

Abash typed an angry email to eXPLosion221. "Whoever you are, you are a complete google bird. I hope you trip and fall and break your arm!"

Abash punched the SEND buttom. But now he felt even *more* embarrassed than he had before.

Suddenly, a message from eXPLosion221 popped up. "I probably won't trip. I know how to put on a *pair* of shoes! LOL!!!"

"Meet me on the playground at 4:00," Abash typed. "I'll show you what two left shoes can do when I kick you in the behind!"

But before he could punch SEND, Abash heard a soft voice behind him. "Take a breath, Abash. Let's talk."

Abash spun around. A-Net and Imp were there.

"Abash, Imp has something that he would like to tell you," A-Net continued.

"I am so sorry, Abash," Imp said quietly. "I didn't erase the picture like you asked, and someone found it and sent it to the whole school."

"But why?" Abash whispered. "Was it something I did?"

"NO WAY, MAN!" shouted Imp.

"Abash, it's not your fault. A genuine cyber-bully is on the loose," explained A-Net. "Cyber-bullies are usually mad at someone or something they can't get back at. So they take their anger out on other people. A cyber-bully thinks that if he makes other Emotes mad, then that will make him feel better."

"Well, it worked!" yelled Abash.

"It's normal to get mad sometimes. But letting a cyber-bully know how you feel is only going to make him stronger," said A-Net. Then she transported away.

"Dude, *you* are the strong one for talking about how you feel instead of trying to get back at this mean old cyber-bully!" Imp said.

That made Abash feel better. He and Imp began to form a plan.

Abash and Imp went to the playground. Joi, Ick, and Mixy came over and said hi.

Suddenly, Boom came running around the corner. But he stopped when he saw Abash and Imp. "What's up?" Boom snarled.

"Let's have a Talkaboutit," Abash replied calmly.

Boom wrinkled his nose. "What in the world is a Talkaboutit?"

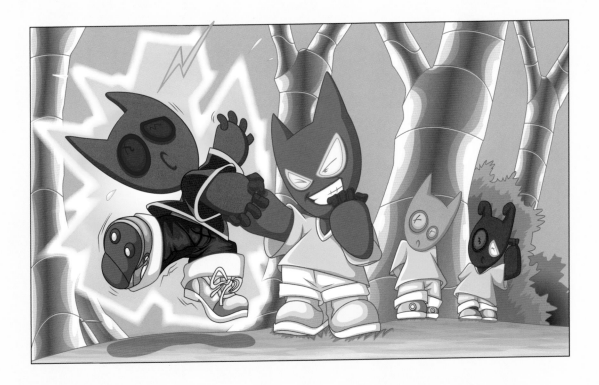

"Sometimes jokes can go too far. Take it from me, I'm the king of practical jokes," said Imp, shaking Boom's hands with a whirlybuzz maker.

"When jokes get out of control, they become bullying, and bullying just isn't funny," added Abash nervously.

"Well, it's pretty funny to me," Boom said loudly.

"WELL IT'S NOT FUNNY TO US!" shouted a group of voices. It was all of the Emotes. And they were looking at Boom.

"I traced your email, Mr. eXPLosion221," Super told Boom. "We know that *you* are the cyber-bully. And it has to stop *now*!"

Boom and Abash had a Talkaboutit while the rest of the Emotes listened. A-Net appeared and hovered over them.

Abash told Boom how he was feeling. Boom listened to every word.

"It just isn't cool to make people feel embarrassed," Abash concluded.

"I'm sorry, Abash," Boom said softly. "I guess I just wanted to distract everyone so that they wouldn't see this." He pointed to his feet.

The other Emotes gasped in surprise. Boom was wearing two right shoes!

Abash and Boom smiled at each other. "Are you thinking what I'm thinking?" Abash asked.

Boom nodded. He handed Abash one right shoe, and Abash handed him one left shoe. All the Emotes cheered.

Out of the corner of his eye, Abash saw a cyber-gopher running into the cyber-forest. He could have sworn it was wearing two left shoes. Abash smiled. "Yup, just another nice, normal, ordinary day."

THE END

WHAT IS CYBER-BULLYING?

Cyber-bullies use the Internet or cell phones to send hurtful messages to people. They might tell secrets, spread rumors, say mean things, or even post pictures as a way to try and make other people feel mad or sad.

BUT WHY WOULD THEY DO THAT? IS IT MY FAULT?

NO! It is NEVER your fault if you are bullied. Most bullies are very sad or mad at something or someone else. Bullies think that making other people sad or mad will make them feel better.

WHAT SHOULD I DO IF I AM CYBER-BULLIED?

Here is the most important thing. Ready? NEVER STRIKE BACK.

If you are bullied, it's normal to feel bad, sad, or mad, but writing an angry reply will only make the cyber-bully want to bully you more. Bullies feel strong when they see other people all fired up. SO, KEEP COOL. Put out their fire by being STRONGER and BRAVER than a bully. Instead, try talking to someone that you can trust. Let a friend, teacher, or parent know how you feel. A good friend can help you decide what the best way to handle the bullying is. Usually the best way to stop a cyber-bully is to IGNORE him.

HERE ARE SOME THINGS TO REMEMBER ABOUT CYBER-BULLYING...

◎ Jokes can go too far. If you send messages that are hurtful and do not respect the feelings of others, you might be a cyber-bully. Be cool and think about other people's feelings, even when you're joking around.

◎ Think before you type. Never send any responses to cyber-bullies until you are calm and can think about what you are typing.

◎ Have a Talkaboutit. Talking about your feelings with your friends and family is ALWAYS a good idea!

◎ Never post or send any information into cyberspace that could be used by someone to bully you.

◎ BE SAFE. Never send ANY personal information into cyberspace — you never know who will find it.

◎ Usually the best way to make bullies stop bullying is to IGNORE THEM.

◎ If you think talking to the bully is the best idea, then don't get angry — and don't go by yourself. Bullies don't like groups of people — they prefer to bully people when they are alone.

◎ Stop going to any blogs or groups where you are being bullied.

◎ Remove anyone who bullies you from all of your buddy lists.

◎ Remember to keep COOL, stay STRONG, and be SMART.

ABOUT THE AUTHORS:

Matt Casper, M.A., MFT. Matt is a licensed Marriage and Family Therapist. He graduated from Duke University, where he studied psychology, religion, and film. He received his master's degree in Marriage and Family Therapy from the California Graduate Institute of Professional Psychology and Psychoanalysis. Matt currently lives in Los Angeles, where he works with people of all ages to help them identify, understand, and express their emotions.

Ted Dorsey is a writer and independent educator living in Los Angeles, California. A graduate of Princeton University, he has written for the stage, film, and television.